# Telling Tales

Compiled by Barbara Ireson

Illustrated by Tony Ross

**RED FOX**

## ACKNOWLEDGEMENTS

Every effort has been made to correctly credit the material reproduced in this book. The publishers apologise if any source is wrongly attributed. The compiler and publishers wish to thank the following for permission to use copyright material in this anthology:

Penguin Books Ltd for 'Excuses, Excuses' by Andrew Matthews from *The Great Sandwich Racket*, published by Blackie.

Barbara Sleigh for 'Miss Peabody' from *West of Widdershins*, published by HarperCollins.

Penguin Books Australia Ltd for 'Next Time Around' by Paul Jennings from *Unbearable!*

Hamish Hamilton for 'My Best Fiend' by Sheila Lavelle from *My Best Fiend*.

Penguin Books for 'Hop o' my Thumb' by René Goscinny from *Nicholas and the Gang*, published by Abelard-Schuman.

Transworld Publishers Ltd for 'The Name is Billy Molloy' by Kathryn Cave from *Many Happy Returns and Other Stories*, published by Corgi Books.

Reed Consumer Books for 'What's For Dinner?' by Robert Swindells from *No More School*, published by Methuen Children's Books.

Penguin Books Ltd for 'The Hidden Horse' by Martin Waddell from *Harriet and the Haunted School*, published by Abelard-Schuman.

David Higham Associates for 'Mr Parker and the Missing Sock' by Nick Warburton from *Mr Parker's Autumn Term*, first published by Hutchinson Children's Books.

# Contents

# Excuses, Excuses

## Andrew Matthews

Not long after the roof blew off Wyvern Copse, Two Red noticed that there was a battle going on. The battle was between Gerry Atkins and Mr Haggerty, Two Red's French Teacher, and it was about homework; or rather, the lack of it.

It was a surprising struggle. Gerry was a pear-shaped boy with brown hair and freckles whose only outstanding quality was his unremarkability; Mr Haggerty was a large man with a mane of white hair, bristling eyebrows and a reputation for prickliness. He was particularly prickly when it came to homework and was Master of the Awkward Question.

'I couldn't do the exercise you set us last night, I didn't understand it, sir,' would be met with, 'Then where is the work you did instead?'

Any pupil honest enough to admit forgetting homework would be given verbs to write out. Mr Haggerty took pains to point out that the verbs were not a punishment but an aid to the memory.

\*

The first time Gerry Atkins failed to do his French, he had a genuine enough excuse – he had been ill when it was set. Mr Haggerty had nodded sympathetically and said that Gerry would have to do double homework to make up for the time he had lost.

Gerry was aggrieved by this.

'It's not fair!' he complained loudly to his mate, Tim Worcester. 'He's punishing me because I was ill! It wasn't my fault!'

'It was in a way,' said Tim. 'You told me it was all those Mexican beans you ate.'

'I was hungry!' Gerry countered. 'I like Mexican beans! I didn't know that eating two lots would turn me into a human aerosol can the next day, did I? Now I've got double French homework because of it! That Haggerty bloke isn't human!'

'Of course he isn't,' Tim agreed. 'He's a teacher.'

Gerry set his jaw and squinted determinedly. 'Well I'm not doing it! He can whistle for his precious homework!'

'But, Gerry!' squeaked Tim. 'It's Mr Haggerty!'

'I know.'

'Winding him up is like juggling with nitroglycerine! Just do the extra work! A quiet life's better than a noisy, painful death!'

'No!' said Gerry. 'This is a matter of principle!'

Battle was joined in the next French lesson. When Mr Haggerty asked for the book to be handed in, Gerry's hand went up in the air like the tail of a cat who has just heard a tin being opened.

'Ah, Atkins!' smiled Mr Haggerty. 'You're about to give in two homeworks, aren't you?'

'No, sir,' said Gerry. 'I haven't done any homework at all, sir.'

Mr Haggerty's smile stayed fixed but his eyes narrowed. 'Why not, Atkins?'

'We had a power cut last night, sir.'

Power cuts had been frequent since the Great October Storm and it was not the first time that Mr Haggerty had dealt with this particular excuse.

'Didn't you have any candles in your house, Atkins?'

'Yes, sir, a box-full, sir!' responded Gerry.

'Then why didn't you do your homework by candle-light?' concluded Mr Haggerty triumphantly.

'Well, sir,' began Gerry, 'the thing is, the box of candles was in the garden shed. My mum sent me out to get them. I was bringing them back into the house when I tripped over and they went flying. It was so dark because of the power cut, I couldn't find them, sir!'

If Mr Haggerty had been a dog, he would have growled; as it was he frowned severely and when he spoke, the temperature of his voice was well below zero.

'I'm going to give you the benefit of the doubt, Atkins, and believe you. This time. You will do both homeworks by Friday and show them to me at the start of the lesson.'

'My granny's coming to stay, sir!' said Gerry hurriedly.

Mr Haggerty looked puzzled. 'A fascinating snippet of information, Atkins, whose relevance, for the moment, eludes me!'

'Well, you see, sir, my granny's a bit funny . . .'

'I don't care if she's an award-winning comedienne, laddie!' roared Mr Haggerty. 'Get those homeworks done, or else!'

In registration on Friday morning, Gerry and Tim were approached by Wayne Armitage, Two Red's wheeler-dealer.

'You done that French then, Atko?' he asked confidentially.

'No.'

Wayne whistled.

'You gotta lotta bottle, kid,' he said. 'Either that or you're a complete wally! Anyway, fancy a little flutter?'

'Flutter?' echoed Gerry.

'You know, a bet!' Wayne explained.

'A bet on what?'

'5p stake,' said Wayne. 'Two-to-one, you gets put in detention. Five-to-one, 'Aggerty drags you straight down to the 'Ead!'

'What if he lets me off?' asked Gerry.

Wayne laughed, ''Aggerty let you off? Ten-to-one chance, mate!'

'Right!' said Gerry, digging in his pocket for a five pence piece. 'You're on!'

The atmosphere was tense at the start of French. All eyes were fixed on Gerry as, with a flourish, he set his exercise book down on Mr Haggerty's table. Mr Haggerty leafed through the book and his eyes bulged.

'What's the meaning of this, Atkins?' he rasped. 'Your homework is still not done!'

'I tried to tell you last time, sir! My granny's staying with us.'

'Atkins,' seethed Mr Haggerty, 'I'm going to ask you a simple question, but I want you to think carefully about your answer, because it could be your last words! What does your grandmother have to do with it?'

'She hates anything to do with France, sir! She suffers from Francophobia.'

'What?' shrieked Mr Haggerty.

'Anything to do with France gives her one of her turns, sir,' said Gerry. 'She trampled the remote control on our telly last year when Delia Smith did a recipe for coq au vin. I can't do any French homework while she's in the house, sir.'

Mr Haggerty tried to speak several times, without success. When his voice eventually emerged, it was strangled, as though he were doing to his vocal cords what he would like to do to Gerry.

'Atkins, when is your grandmother leaving?'

'Tonight, sir.'

'Very well. Over the weekend, you'll do the two homeworks you owe me, plus the one I'm setting this lesson. You'll show them to me on Monday. And . . .

9

Atkins?'

'Sir?'

'If you are taken ill, dictate your homework to a nurse!' snapped Mr Haggerty. 'If the illness proves fatal, dictate it to a medium!'

At the end of the lesson, Wayne Armitage paid Gerry fifty pence. He was grinning broadly as he did it.

'Magic!' he exclaimed admiringly.

'What are you so happy about?' Gerry demanded. 'Does losing money appeal to your sense of humour, or something?'

'Who's losin' money?' beamed Wayne. 'Twenty kids in our class bet that you'd get put in detention! I'm 50p up on the deal! I'm openin' another book for Monday. Two-to-one you do the 'omework, ten-to-one you don't do it and you gets a detention!'

'What if I don't do it and I get away with it?' Gerry asked curiously.

'Impossible!' gasped Wayne.

'Like to bet?'

'Bookies never bet!' said Wayne scornfully. 'It's a mug's game!'

In registration on Monday morning, Gerry was the centre of attention.

'I feel quietly confident,' he told Tim. 'I've been in training all over the weekend and I think I'm fully prepared.'

'I couldn't eat this morning!' Tim confessed. 'I kept on thinking about what Mr Haggerty was going to do to you. It put me off my breakfast!'

'I had porridge, kippers and toast!' said Gerry nonchalantly. 'I got a couple of Mars bars down on the way to school as well!'

'No point dying on an empty stomach, I suppose!' said Tim.

Gerry smiled enigmatically.

The air in the French room was electric. The spectators took their seats and a buzz of excitement went around as Gerry Atkins, one of the contenders, took his place at the back of the class. The buzz died to an expectant silence as Mr Haggerty entered and the crowd prepared themselves for a no-holds-barred contest.

'Take out your exercise books and turn to your homework!' commanded Mr Haggerty.

In the ensuing shuffle, Gerry's arm lifted into the air. 'Please sir, may I leave the room, sir!' he whispered desperately.

'No you may not, Atkins! Too much for you, eh, laddie?' sneered Mr Haggerty. 'Lost the stomach for it? Open that exercise book.'

'But . . . sir . . .'

'Do as you're told!' bawled Mr Haggerty.

Gerry opened his French book on the table. 'Sir . . .' he whimpered.

'It's no use being pathetic!' boomed Mr Haggerty, advancing. 'There's no escape this time, is there, laddie? I've got you right . . .'

Gerry was sick – gloriously and spectacularly sick – all over his French book.

The next morning, Mr Haggerty sent for Gerry during registration and met him in the French Department Office.

'All right, Atkins!' he sighed. 'You win. I want to call a truce.'

'Sir?' said Gerry innocently.

'We'll forget about the homeworks you owe me, but as of this Friday, you'll do your French like everybody else, or I'll take you to the Headmaster. Is that clear?'

'Yes, sir.'

Mr Haggerty handed over a new exercise book. 'No more excuses, Atkins?'

'No, sir!'

'Right!' smiled Mr Haggerty. 'When you get back to your form base, send Wayne Armitage over to me. I want to collect my winnings.'

'Winnings, sir?' frowned Gerry.

'Yes,' said Mr Haggerty. 'I bet 2p that you'd get away with it yesterday. Wayne offered odds of a hundred-to-one. He owes me two pounds.'

# Miss Peabody

## Barbara Sleigh

Once upon a time there was a teacher called Miss
Peabody, and a class called Lower 3a.

After the strange things that happened one summer
term, Lower 3a were never quite sure if Miss Peabody
was a witch, but they decided they had better be a little
bit careful, just in case. You never know with witches.
Lower 3a was just the kind of class which can make
teachers very cross indeed in the shortest possible time.

Miss Peabody could have told them exactly how the
strange things came about. But of course she never
did. It all began with her headaches. Usually her lessons
were interesting enough to keep any class from being
naughty: especially history. But if she had one of her
headaches they became very dull indeed, and then of
course, Lower 3a enlivened them with all the old
dodges. They talked and giggled: they made long visits
to the cloakroom to fetch handkerchiefs which were
not there: they put up-ended drawing pins on one
another's chairs, and ate a special kind of wine gum
that they thought, mistakenly, could be sucked without

anyone knowing.

This particular summer term the Mayor had offered a prize to the group in any school which made the best model illustrating something in history. Miss Peabody got quite excited. So did Lower 3a. They began to make a model of old London Bridge, with paper mashed up in paste, and poster paint, and shiny crinkled paper for the River Thames.

Lower 3a were working very hard and Miss Peabody was pleased with them, when one of her headaches started, and then another, and another. And from a class of keen young model-makers, Lower 3a became a giggling, inattentive rabble. Paint water was upset, up-ended drawing pins appeared all over the place, and the sweet shop completely ran out of wine gums because they bought so many. Of course the model of old London Bridge began to suffer.

'I shall *have* to go to the doctor about these head-aches,' said Miss Peabody to herself. 'But not to Doctor Simson this time. Supposing Bobby Simson saw me sitting in the surgery? The whole of Lower 3a would know about it in the morning, and goodness knows how it might make them giggle! I shall take a bus ticket to the end of the bus route and go to the first doctor I can find.'

When she left the bus Miss Peabody had to walk quite a long way, so that it was dusk before she found a doctor. There was not enough light to read his name on the brass plate outside, but there was a red light over the door.

'How old-fashioned!' said Miss Peabody to herself. For that is how doctors showed their trade a long time ago.

The doctor sat at his desk. There was only the light of a reading lamp in the surgery, but she could see that three of the walls were covered with ancient books, with powdery leather bindings. There were, as well, some scales and a sight-testing card, and hanging over the desk, to her surprise, was a stuffed alligator.

'How very odd!' said Miss Peabody to herself. 'Almost as if . . .'

'As if what?' repeated the doctor looking up for the first time, and although he was the oldest old man Miss Peabody had ever seen, his eyes were surprisingly young and bright. 'If there is a stuffed toad in the science room of Birch Road Junior School, why should I not have a stuffed alligator in my surgery? Now about these headaches of yours . . .' Miss Peabody gave a little gasp, for she had never said a word out loud about either headaches or alligators or Birch Road Junior School, but the doctor went on: 'It seems that children are much the same as they have always been.'

'But Lower 3a . . .' began Miss Peabody.

'I know,' broke in the doctor. 'Drawing pins and wine gums and the rest. I think a little Wishing Tonic may be what you need, and no doubt it will do Lower 3a a little good as well.'

As he spoke he wrote on his prescription pad, in the

usual doctor's unreadable writing, and handed the little slip of paper to Miss Peabody. 'Good day to you,' he said. 'Next patient, please!'

The chemist looked a little puzzled when she handed him the prescription.

'I don't think I've ever been asked for this before,' he said. But the medicine looked quite ordinary when he had made it up. It was in two tiny bottles. The label on one said: 'An egg shell full to be taken after breakfast.' The liquid was red. The other was green as grass. The label on this just said 'The Antidote'.

'To undo the first medicine, I suppose. How very odd!'

Miss Peabody could hardly wait for next day. She woke with the worst possible headache. The medicine hissed slightly when she poured it into the newly washed shell of her breakfast egg, and a little nervously she shut her eyes and swallowed it down. It was sweet and syrupy, and it sent a tingling glow from her toes to her finger tips, but when she opened her eyes her head hurt as much as ever.

'How I wish it would cure the pain!' said Miss Peabody.

And at once it did. Her headache had quite gone – 'As if by magic!' she said. And then she caught sight of the clock. 'Goodness, how late it is! And it's pouring with rain. I wish I was at school!'

And at once she was: sitting in her desk in Lower 3a classroom, breathing a little quickly, and with her hair rather blown about. Willy Brown and Nora Smith, who had come to school early to arrange some up-ended drawing pins, were staring at her with their mouths open. Miss Peabody saw what they were up to, but she said to herself: 'It's happened twice! I said, "I wish . . ." and my headache went, and I said it again and it whisked me here! It *must* be magic!' Aloud she said: 'How splendid of you to come early to get on with your work, Nora and Willy. When you've picked up all those drawing pins someone seems to have spilled, you may fill the paint pots with water for me.'

'Yes, Miss Peabody,' said Nora and Willy meekly.

It was only when she reached the door that she realised that she was still wearing her bedroom slippers. They were scarlet with yellow pom-poms. Nora was staring at them with round eyes, but she did not giggle.

18

Miss Peabody wished the magic had given her time to change. It was all rather difficult to explain when she had to borrow a pair of gym shoes from the gym teacher.

Lessons began as usual. Although Lower 3a felt that there was something different about Miss Peabody, being naughty had become a habit. When they were doing sums there were spurts of giggling, and presently there was the unmistakable smell of someone sucking wine gums.

'Who is eating sweets?' asked Miss Peabody.

Barry Jones and Sara Robinson put up their hands. Several others looked a little uncomfortable.

'Put them in the wastepaper basket at once,' said Miss Peabody. 'You know, if all the sweets this class has eaten during lessons this term were put end to end, you would be surprised how far they would reach. I wish you could see them!'

And at once they could. There was a line of sweets stretching from Miss Peabody's desk, down the classroom and round the corner, right to the door. There were wine gums and jelly babies and chocolate bars, and liquorice bootlaces and hundreds-and-thousands and peppermint lumps and assorted toffees galore.

'Leave them where they are,' said Miss Peabody. 'And perhaps the sight of them will make you feel a little ashamed!'

There was no more giggling. Lower 3a went on with their work without a sound.

Ten minutes later Mr Hammock the headmaster opened the door.

'Miss Peabody,' he said coldly. 'There is a trail of sweets leading from your classroom right down the passage and round the corner to the door of my study. I suppose Lower 3a is responsible?'

Lower 3a all held their breaths as they waited for Miss Peabody's answer.

'Oh, no,' she said after a moment's pause. 'It was entirely my doing. A little experiment in – er, arithmetic.'

Lower 3a breathed again. Good old Poddy, they thought! They had been rather beastly to her lately, but she hadn't given them away!

'I think such practical experiments should be carried out inside the classroom in future,' said Mr Hammock, and stalked away on his long legs.

'Barry and Sara, please take the wastepaper basket and collect all the sweets in the passage,' said Miss Peabody. 'And don't eat a single one! I shall know if you do.' (Goodness knows what they might turn into if they did eat them!) 'How thoughtless this magic business is!' she went on to herself. 'Bringing me to school in my bedroom slippers, and no hat or coat on a wet day like this, and taking the sweets to Mr Hammock's door, of all people! I shall have to be very careful of saying "I wish", without thinking.'

But it was more easily said than done.

Miss Peabody was careful for several days, and then,

in the middle of a lesson on geography, a button came off Susan Pollock's cuff. John Tomkins, who sat next to her, already had a shirt button in his pencil box, so that a game of Tiddlywinks seemed the natural thing to do with them. One or two others thought it rather a good idea, and if they had not a button handy, they pulled one off where it would not show. They were so busy about it that John and Sara did not see Miss Peabody standing behind them.

'Give me those buttons, please,' she said. Then hearing the snick of another Tiddlywinks player she added: 'I wish to have all the buttons in the room on my desk, please!'

She meant of course all the *loose* buttons in the room, but that was not what she had said. There was a pause, and then the air was filled with a number of little poppings, like the patter of small hard things falling like rain on the lid of Miss Peabody's desk.

'That wishing magic again!' she said to herself, and went on wildly: 'Counting fifteen buttons to each child, that makes 775!'

And then the bell went for the next lesson.

'You must go to the gym now,' she said aloud. 'And when you come back you can sew them all on again.'

'But we can't go to gym like this!' said George almost tearfully, holding up his trousers with both hands.

Miss Peabody looked at Lower 3a, all holding their clothes together, without a single button between them, and said: 'Perhaps you're right. Instead of gym we shall

21

just have to have a sewing lesson. Boys as well as girls.'

But there was worse to come. It was Miss Peabody's turn for dinner duty that day with the whole school, together with Miss Price. It was boiled cod, white and watery. George was sitting, on her right, and Patty, who hated fish in any form, on her left. To distract Miss Peabody, while Patty got rid of her cod, George said: 'Miss Peabody, what did people eat in the days of old London Bridge?'

'An Elizabethan feast, you mean? Well, I suppose it would taste a little odd to us,' said Miss Peabody, turning to George, while Patty thankfully shovelled the cod into her handkerchief. 'But I expect it would be delicious when you got used to it. I only wish you could taste one!'

The noise of 120 children talking, and the clatter of 120 knives and forks stopped as suddenly as though it had been turned off by a tap. The checked tablecloths were gone, and the thick white plates and the mangled pieces of cod. Instead, in the centre of the long polished table that had taken the place of the chipped deal one provided by the school, was a large model of the school crest, an owl in a mortarboard, all made of sugar. In front of each boy and girl was a shining pewter plate and a large tankard, and up and down the table were huge dishes of wonderful fruit: peaches and cherries, oranges and strawberries. There were sugar plums and suckets, and piles of sweetmeats, and marzipan that made the mouth water. The door opened and the kitchen staff filed in, looking a little puzzled, but bearing great dishes on high. Miss Peabody rose excitedly.

'Roast peacock!' she cried. 'And venison pastry, and sucking pig and marrowbone pie! A real Elizabethan feast, dears, this is wonderful! The only way to teach history! Why did I not think of it before? Come along, children, eat it up!'

'But we've no knives or forks!' said Sally Wilkinson.

'Of course not, dear!' said Miss Peabody. 'Use your fingers! That's what everyone did in the days of old London Bridge! Eat up your sucking pig, Henry! And Pamela, no jumbals or suckets till you have finished your nice stewed pike! I'm sure it's delicious, cooked in wine and cream. Those black things it is stuffed with,

William? Why, prunes, of course!'

Gingerly, Birch Road Junior School tasted the strange food before them, and as they found most of it good they took heart and tucked in manfully, while Miss Peabody urged them on. She had quite forgotten Miss Price, who suddenly took her firmly by the arm, at the same time holding up an enormous tankard.

'What is the liquid in this?' she asked. Miss Peabody peered and smelt and tasted, and then she said impatiently: 'Malmsey wine, of course ... Well no, perhaps they had better not drink that. Billy dear, put that tankard down!'

'But Miss Peabody, it all looks so indigestible, don't you think?' said Miss Price. 'Tomorrow...'

'Tomorrow,' said Miss Peabody triumphantly, 'I shall take the whole of Lower 3a to Elizabethan England! What an opportunity!'

Miss Peabody was so excited by the idea that she did not notice Miss Price hurry from the room. Fifteen minutes later the dishes were almost bare, and Birch Road Juniors, unbelievably sticky and very full indeed, were languidly eating the last of the sugar owl, when the door opened and Mr Hammock came in, followed by Miss Price, and Mrs Honey who cooked the school dinners. Mrs Honey was in tears.

'I never did, sir!' she was saying. 'Cod I cooked for today! Boiled with parsley sauce. Not them horrible messes!'

24

She pointed to the remains of the peacock and the marrowbone pie.

Now Miss Peabody was very sorry to think that she had caused Mrs Honey distress. Many times she had made Miss Peabody a nice strong cup of tea, when she had a headache. Had the magic done it again?

'Please don't cry, Mrs Honey,' she said. 'It was entirely my doing.'

'Then,' said Mr Hammock icily, 'I'm very sorry to hear it! As you know I am always in favour of practical teaching, but this is carrying things too far!'

'But, Mr Hammock, don't you see?' said Miss Peabody. 'These children have had a history lesson they will never forget! How I wish I was a child again with them . . .'

She stopped, her hand over her mouth. But it was too late. Before the astonished eyes of Mr Hammock, Miss Price, Mrs Honey, and all the pupils of Birch Road Junior School, she began to shrink. She herself felt as if she was going down, rather too quickly, in a lift which stopped with a jolt, and left her staring at the bottom button of Mr Hammock's waistcoat, instead of his surprised blue eyes. Then she noticed a chilliness about her knees. With a gasp of dismay she watched her sensible tweed skirt shrink and fade into a very short gym tunic. Something was tickling her neck. She put her hand up and felt the ribbons on the end of her two rather thin plaits.

Mr Hammock's face, now tilted down at her, looked

dazed.

'I can't quite remember the class you are in, my dear,' he said uncertainly. 'But I will see you in my study. Immediately!' he added, pulling himself together.

Miss Peabody rushed from the dining-room, but not to Mr Hammock's study. She dashed down the passage and out of the front door. Along the drive she ran, her plump knees twinkling, along the High Street, down Percy Avenue, with one thing only in her mind, the second bottle of medicine! She was not trusting to any more wishes. Down her own road she pelted, through the front door and up the stairs to her room. She snatched up the bottle with its liquid, green as grass, and tossed it all off in one gulp. It burnt her throat and made her cough. She shut her eyes and counted twenty. The same curious 'lift' feeling began again, but this time going up. Then she opened her eyes and looked in the mirror. Never had she gazed at her own ordinary but grown-up reflection with such pleasure! Then she took a deep breath – and wished she was back at school again. Nothing happened. Miss Peabody gave a sigh of relief.

A few of the Birch Road Junior School children were rather unwell in the night, but nobody ever referred to that afternoon again: not even Mr Hammock. Lower 3a did win the Mayor's Prize after all. Miss Peabody never had another headache and Lower 3a were seldom naughty, at least, not in Miss Peabody's lessons. As far as I know there has been no more magic at Birch

Road Junior School: though there was a rumour that Winifred Potts had seen Miss Peabody whirl past the cloakroom window on a broomstick late one evening, when she had been kept in. But you know how stories get about in school.

# Next Time Around

### Paul Jennings

It all started when I was reading a comic called . . .
what was it again . . .? I forget now. Anyway, this comic
reckoned you could hypnotise chickens by staring them
in the eye and making chook noises.

Well, it was worth a try. See, Dad had this prize chook
named Rastus. It used to win ribbons at the show. He
kept it in a cage in the garage and gave it nothing but
the best to eat. Dad loved Rastus.

It was smart chook. I have to admit that. You probably
won't believe me when I tell you that Rastus could
understand English. 'Rastus,' Dad would say. 'Count to
four.' Rastus would peck the cage four times. No kid-
ding. It could go all the way up to twenty-two without
making a mistake. It sure was brainy.

Anyway, I wanted to see if the comic was right. It
would be great to hypnotise a chook. I sneaked out to
the garage and let Rastus onto the floor. Then I did
what it said in the comic. I stared straight into Rastus'
eyes. 'Puck, puck, puck, puck,' I said.

Rastus didn't take any notice. He just started scratching around on the ground. It didn't work. Things in comics never do. Still, I decided to give it one more try. This time I changed pitch. I made my voice higher. More like a chook's. 'Puck, puck, puck, puck,' I went.

Well, you wouldn't believe it. The silly chook froze like a statue. Its eyes went all glassy. It stood as still as a rock. Not a blink. Not a movement. It was out to it. Hypnotised. I had done it. Fantastic.

I walked around and around the staring chook. I poked it with my finger. It still didn't move. I grinned to myself. I could hypnotise chooks. Maybe this would make me famous. I could go on the stage. Or the TV. People would pay good money to see the boy who could put a chook into a trance.

Still and all, Dad wasn't going to like it much. He wouldn't win many ribbons with a chicken that just stood and stared.

The back door banged. I could hear Dad packing his fishing rod in the car.

I clicked my fingers at the chook. 'Okay, Rastus,' I said. 'You can snap out of it now.'

Rastus didn't move.

I tried something different. 'When I say bananas,' I said to Rastus, 'you will wake up. You will feel happy and well. You will not remember anything that has happened.'

I took a deep breath. 'Bananas,' I said.

Rastus stared to the front like a solid, feathered

29

soldier.

I picked him up and looked into his eyes. 'Speak to me, Rastus,' I said. 'Puck, puck, puck.' I gave him a vigorous shake.

Rastus was rigid. The rotten rooster was out to it.

Dad's footsteps came towards the garage. 'Oh no,' I said.

I grabbed Rastus and my school bag and nicked out of the back door. Dad was going to be mad when he found out that Rastus had gone. But not as mad as he would be if he knew what I'd done. I wasn't even supposed to go anywhere near the bloomin' chook. And if I couldn't get it out of its trance it might die of starvation.

I made my way slowly to school with the frozen fowl tucked under my arm. Its glassy eyes stared ahead without blinking.

'What have you got there?' said a loud voice. It was Splinter, my best mate.

'It's Rastus,' I said.

Splinter whistled. 'Wow. How did he die?'

'He's not dead. He's hypnotised. I can't bring him round.'

By now we had reached the school gate. 'Pull the other one,' said Splinter.

'No, it's true,' I said. 'I'm a hypnotist. I did it.'

'Okay,' said Splinter. 'Hypnotise me then.'

I looked around the school ground. Kids were staring

30

at me because I was standing there with a bit of petrified poultry under my arm. I could feel my face going red. 'All right,' I said. 'I will. But first I have to hide Rastus.'

We found a little trap-door under one of the portable classrooms and hid Rastus inside. He looked kind of sad, staring out at us from the dark.

Splinter stretched himself out on a bench. 'Right,' he said. 'Get on with it. Put me in a trance.'

A group of kids gathered around. They were all scoffing like mad. They wanted to see me hypnotise Splinter. They didn't really think I could do it. Neither did I. A chook was one thing. But a person was another.

I took a silver pen from my pocket. 'Follow the tip of this pen with your eyes,' I said.

Splinter did as he was told. He had a big grin on his face. His eyes went from left to right like someone watching a tennis match. Suddenly the grin disappeared. Splinter's eyes went glassy. He stared to the front. Splinter was as solid as a statue.

Was he fooling? I didn't really know. I couldn't be sure. He was the sort of kid who was always playing jokes. 'You are a chook,' I said.

Splinter jumped to his feet and started crowing like a rooster. He was very good. He sounded just like the real thing; not like someone trying to copy a rooster. The kids around all gasped. They were impressed.

But I wasn't sure about it. I had a feeling that Splinter was tricking me. I had to find out. 'Splinter,' I said.

'When I count to three you will be your old self. You will not be a chook any more. But whenever you hear the word "no" you will be a chicken again for thirty seconds.'

Splinter was just opening his mouth to start crowing again. I had to be quick. 'One, two, three,' I said. Splinter shook his head and blinked. He was back to normal.

The school bell rang and everyone made for the doors.

'What happened?' asked Splinter. He really didn't seem to remember. I smiled to myself. I was a hypnotist. From now on nobody could give me any cheek. I would make them think they were worms. Or maggots. Life was looking good.

But not for long.

We went into the first class. Maths. With Mr Spiggot. He sure was a mean teacher. If you hadn't done your homework you had to stand up and be yelled at. Or do a Saturday morning detention. Three girls were expelled because of him. Just for giving cheek.

Mr Spiggot looked at me. 'Have you done your homework, Robertson?' he growled.

I looked at my shoes. I was in trouble. 'No,' I answered.

'No?' he yelled.

At that very moment Splinter jumped to his feet as if someone had just switched him on. He walked around the class pecking at the floor like a chicken.

'Puck, puck, puck,' he said. The class gasped. Some kids tried to smother a laugh. Splinter was in big trouble. You couldn't fool around in front of Mr Spiggot and get away with it.

Mr Spiggot started to go red in the face. I tried to figure out what was going on. Then I realised. Mr Spiggot and I had said 'no'. We put Splinter into a trance. Just like I'd told him. Splinter really did think he was a chook.

I can tell you one thing. It was the longest thirty seconds of my life. And there was nothing I could do except watch poor Splinter scratch around on the floor in front of the whole class.

Suddenly Splinter stopped. The thirty seconds was up. He looked around with a silly expression. Everyone was laughing. Except Mr Spiggot. He looked straight at me. He knew Splinter was my mate.

'Right,' he said in a very quiet voice. 'You two think you can get out of your homework by acting the fool.' He walked over to his desk and picked up two sheets of paper. He gave us one each.

I groaned. It was Maths homework. Twenty hard problems.

Splinter didn't know what was going on. 'Why?' he asked. 'I haven't done anything.'

'No?' said Mr Spiggot. 'What . . .'

He didn't finish the sentence. As soon as Mr Spiggot said the word 'no', Splinter went back to thinking he was a chicken. He hopped up onto the front desk and squatted down. He put his elbows out like wings and flapped them. Then he sort of bounced up and down. He thought he was a chook laying an egg. 'Puck, puck, puck, puck,' he went.

Everyone packed up. The whole class was in fits. Mr Spiggot picked up two more sheets of sums. He held one out under Splinter's nose. Splinter pecked at his hand with his teeth. Just like a broody hen. Peck, peck, peck. 'Ouch,' shouted Mr Spiggot. He shook his hand and jumped up and down.

Splinter was still trying to lay an egg. Suddenly he stopped. The thirty seconds was up. He blinked. He stood up on the desk. Mr Spiggot was so furious that he couldn't speak. He staggered back to the desk and grabbed a handful of problem sheets. He gave us another one each.

'You two boys can leave my class,' he choked. 'And if those sums are not all finished, CORRECTLY, by tomorrow morning you will both be expelled from the school.'

It was no good trying to explain. He wouldn't believe me. And he might say 'no' again at any minute. We walked sadly out of the room and into the yard.

We made for the portable classroom. Rastus was still there – in a trance. I put him under my arm and we started walking home. It was raining and water dripped down our backs.

'Listen,' I said to Splinter. 'I have to put you into a trance. To stop you going into your chicken act every time I say "no".'

I tried to stop myself saying the last word. 'No.' Too late. Splinter started to scratch around on the footpath. Clucking and pecking. A couple of snails were making their way across the footpath.

Splinter was hungry.

He took a snail between his teeth and hit it on the ground. Then he swallowed it in one gulp. He did the same to another and another. 'Oh no!' I yelled. Splinter was eating live snails. He looked around for more.

I had to do something. Quick. Before the thirty seconds were up. 'When I count to three,' I yelled. 'You will be your old self again. You will not be a chook when anyone says "no".' Then I added something else, just to be on the safe side. 'You will not remember anything about being a chook.' I took a deep breath. 'One, two, three.'

It worked straight away. Better than I thought. Splinter blinked. And winked. He rubbed his eyes. 'What happened?' he asked.

I didn't get a chance to answer him. Rastus flapped out of my arms and squawked crossly. He was his old self again. 'Rastus came out of his trance when I counted to three,' I shouted. 'It was the numbers. He understands numbers.'

Rastus looked up at me as if to agree. Then he pecked the ground three times.

Poor old Splinter wasn't interested in the chook. He waved the sheets of sums in my face. 'We have to do all these by tomorrow,' he groaned. 'Or we're dead meat. My parents will murder me if I'm expelled from school.'

'Come round to my place after tea,' I said. 'We'll stay up all night and work on them.'

Splinter walked home. He dragged his feet as he went. I knew how he was feeling. And it was all my fault.

Mum and Dad were going out that night and I had to mind the baby. 'Mum,' I said. 'Splinter and I have to do homework. I can't mind the baby.'

'Rubbish,' said Mum. 'She'll be asleep. You just want to play records. Homework? That'll be the day.' She went off laughing loudly to herself. I couldn't tell her about the sums. Or being expelled if we didn't finish them. It would be like throwing wood on a bushfire.

The baby was asleep in her bassinet. She was only eighteen months old. But boy was she fat. She'd only just started to walk. She spent all day eating.

'Here's Splinter,' said Mum. She showed him into the lounge room. 'Make sure you don't make too much noise.' She kissed me goodbye even though Splinter was there. Talk about embarrassing.

The baby snored away making sucking noises. We sat down at the table and tried to work out the answer to the first sum. It was something about water running into a bath at two litres a minute and out of the plug at half a litre a minute. You had to work out how long it would take to fill the bath.

'Strike,' said Splinter. 'How do you do it?'

'Search me,' I said. I looked at all the other sums. There were fifty altogether. Real hard ones.

'We'll never do it,' said Splinter.

My heart sank. I knew he was right. Tomorrow we would be expelled from school. We tried and tried for about an hour. But it was no good. We couldn't even work out one answer.

Splinter suddenly threw the papers on the floor. 'I'm sick of this,' he said. 'We might as well do something else.'

This is when Splinter had his brainwave. 'I was watching this show once,' he said. 'About a hypnotist. He could take people back in time. To earlier lives.'

'What do you mean?' I said.

He stared at me. 'Well, this bloke reckoned that everyone has lived before. Only you can't remember it. When you die, you get born again as someone else. If you were really good you might end up being born as a king or something. If you were bad in a past life you might come back as a rat.'

'I don't believe it,' I said.

Splinter was always wanting an adventure. 'Let's give it a try,' he said. 'You hypnotise me and see if I can tell you about an earlier life.'

I didn't want to do it. We were in enough trouble already. But in the end Splinter talked me into it.

'You are feeling sleepy,' I told him. Straight away Splinter started to nod off. I was getting better and better at this hypnotism lark. 'You are going back,' I went on. 'Back to your earlier life. You are going back twenty years. It is the fifth of April at eight o'clock. Who are you?'

There was a long silence. Splinter had his eyes closed. He didn't say anything. He just sat there. It wasn't working.

Then something creepy happened. It made the hairs stand up on the top of my head. Splinter opened his mouth and spoke in a slow, deep voice. It wasn't his voice. It was the speech of a man. 'I am John Rivett,' he said.

It was amazing. I had taken him back in time. To an earlier life. I asked him what he did for a job.

'Fireman,' he said loudly.

'How old are you?'

'Thirty two.'

He was answering my questions very seriously. I wanted to know more. This is when I made my big mistake. 'What are you doing now?' I asked. 'At this very minute?'

'Fire,' Splinter shouted. 'No time to talk. Must put out the fire.' He sat bolt upright. His eyes were wild and staring. He ran over to the sink and filled up a jug of water. Then he threw it at the wall. It ran down Mum's best wallpaper and onto the floor.

'Stop,' I yelled. But it was no good. Splinter was back in an earlier life. He thought the house was on fire. I grabbed him by the arm but he was too strong. He had the power of a grown man. He brushed me aside as if I was a baby and ran outside.

To get the hosepipe.

'When I count to three . . .' I shouted. But it was useless. He wasn't listening. He dragged the hose into the lounge and started squirting the walls. And the sofa. And the carpet. The room was soon swirling with water. I tried to grab him but he was just too strong for me.

He kept shouting something about getting the baby out before the flames reached her. I grabbed the baby and ran into the back yard. Splinter had gone wild. He was wetting everything. He really thought the house was on fire. I had to stop him. But how? There was no one to help.

Or was there?

I stared down at the baby. It was sucking its knuckles and dribbling as usual. 'Baby,' I said. 'You are feeling sleepy. You are going back to another life. It is ten years ago on the third of November. Who are you? What is your name?'

The baby did nothing for a minute or so. Then it sat straight up in its bassinet. It boomed at me with this enormous deep voice. 'Lightning Larry,' said the baby. 'World Heavyweight Boxing Champion.'

'Please help me,' I said to the baby. 'Stop that maniac Splinter from flooding out the house.'

The baby jumped out of the bassinet and headed for the door. Splinter looked in amazement at the baby striding across the lawn. He didn't want an infant to get into a house that he thought was burning down. He slammed the door. The baby let fly with an enormous kick and knocked the door off its hinges.

I groaned. The house was being wrecked. The baby strode across the room to Splinter. Her nappy waggled as she walked. She drew back her arm, gave an enormous leap, and punched Splinter fair on the jaw. He dropped like a felled tree. Out to it.

The baby picked Splinter up and held him above her head. She carried him out to me and dumped him on the grass. 'How's that?' she boomed.

It was scary listening to that enormous voice coming out of such a tiny mouth. The baby gave a wicked grin and held her hands up like a boxer in a ring. 'Still the champ,' she shouted.

Splinter was starting to come round. He sat up and rubbed his jaw. 'When I count to three,' I said to both of them. 'You will forget everything that happened.'

And they did. The baby went back to being a baby and started to bawl. Splinter looked at the fractured door. 'Gee,' he said. 'You're in big trouble.'

And I was. Mum and Dad were furious when they got home. They wouldn't stop going on about it. You know the sort of thing. On and on and on. They wouldn't believe that the baby kicked the door down. Wouldn't even let me start to explain about hypnosis. 'These lies just make it worse, lad,' said Dad.

Splinter was sent home in disgrace. I was sent to bed.

In the morning I woke up and hoped that it had all been a nightmare. But it hadn't. The sheets of unanswered sums were still on the floor.

When I got to school Splinter and I would be expelled. Dad and Mum would blow their tops. Life wasn't worth living.

I walked out of the door towards my doom. 'Make sure you behave yourself at school,' said Mum. I didn't answer.

I went out to check on Rastus. I stayed with him for so long that I made myself late for school.

Maths was the first class as usual. Mr Spiggot was just getting started. I rushed in right at the last minute.

'Right,' said Mr Spiggot in a low voice. 'Stand up, you two. Have you done your homework? Finished those sums?'

'No,' whispered Splinter.

'Yes we have,' I said. 'We worked on them together.'

41

'Okay, let's see,' said Mr Spiggot. He read out the first sum. The problem about the bath water. Then he looked at me for the answer.

'Three minutes,' I said. Mr Spiggot raised an eyebrow. I was right.

Mr Spiggot read out the next sum. It was about how many kilometres a car could travel in two days at a certain speed. 'Five hundred and two,' I said.

'Correct,' said Mr Spiggot. He read out all the sums. And I answered every one correctly. We were saved. You should have seen the look on Splinter's face.

Well, that's about all. We didn't get expelled but I was grounded for a month by Mum for all the water damage.

Looking back on it now, I would have to say that using hypnotism is not a good idea. I'm never doing it again. Never. It caused too much trouble.

If you asked me what was the worst bit, I would say it was when Splinter ate the snails. That was terrible.

And the best bit? Well, that was probably when I stopped to check on Rastus on the way to school that day. It was a great idea to send him back to an earlier life. It turned out that the silly chook had been a Maths teacher in a previous existence. I just read him the problems and he pecked out the answers. As easy as anything.

But I'll tell you what. Mr Spiggot's a Maths teacher. He'd better watch out. I reckon he'll probably be coming back as a flea next time around.

# Mr Parker and the Missing Sock

Nick Warburton

The one thing Mr Parker always insists on when he reads stories is silence. He can't stand the slightest noise. And the worst sound of all, to Mr Parker's ears, is the sound of Mrs Stubbs opening the classroom door.

When Mr Parker began to read *The Borrowers*, he took a deep breath and closed his eyes.

'Relax,' he said. 'Let's all be at peace. Listening and thinking – thinking and listening – for which we must have – Absolute – Golden – Silence.'

And the children gathered round Mr Parker and there was silence.

Then – the door flew open. It banged against the wall and shuddered.

In she came with a hearty shout: Mrs Stubbs! Like a train from a tunnel: Mrs Stubbs! Like a brick through a window: Mrs Stubbs! Waving a sock above her head and crying: 'Anyone here lost a sock? A missing sock? A single sock, colour of blue! One last chance for the missing SOCK!'

Mr Parker kept himself perfectly still. His eyes

43

remained closed and only his nostrils seemed to move, very slightly in and out, like an undersea plant.

And that was the start of The Battle of the Missing Sock between Mrs Stubbs and Mr Parker.

*One* – Mrs Stubbs was in her office counting dinner money, a job she enjoyed. All the money was in neat little piles on her desk and she was just about to add the last sum.

'And forty-two fives makes two pounds and ten pence,' she muttered to herself. 'And one hundred and eleven pounds and sixty pence plus two pounds and ten pence makes . . .'

Then in burst Mr Parker.

'A sock! A missing sock!' he cried with a flourish. 'One last chance for THE MISSING SOCK!'

And he dumped the sock on Mrs Stubbs' desk, scattering coins all over the place. So the counting had to begin again.

*Two* – Mr Parker was about to open his register the

44

next morning when he caught a whiff of something strange. He wrinkled his nose and sniffed. Oh no, he thought. It can't be . . . but it was. Pinned to his register was that sock, staring up at him like an old, lost fish.

**Three** – Mr Parker's turn. He tiptoed to the Cloakroom and hid the sock in Mrs Stubbs' woolly hat. At the end of the day she put on her coat and pulled her hat firmly down on her head. The sock peeped out from behind her ear and it stayed there till she noticed someone giggling on the bus.

'Right,' she said. 'Just wait till tomorrow.'

**Four** – At lunch time the next day Mr Parker collected a bowl of semolina and a spoon – a large bowl with plenty of lumpy semolina, just as Mr Parker likes it.

'Very lumpy today,' he said with a smile. 'Perfect.'

Then he looked at his bowl. Strange he thought. Only one lump. A large single lump, colour of blue. The missing sock!

'This has gone too far,' said Mr Parker and he marched the bowl of semolina, with the sock in it, to

Mrs Stubbs' office. 'She can have the lot,' he said.

But just as he was about to hurl it through the door, he stopped and thought.

That's odd, he thought. A sock in semolina. But not just any sock. A blue sock, a sock *well-known* to him.

He looked down at his feet.

Two legs with two feet in two brown shoes . . . but only one blue sock.

'Oh dear,' Mr Parker said to himself. 'It must be mine.'

When he put the missing sock on again his feet didn't feel quite right. One foot was cool and dry and the other warm and wet. They felt so uncomfortable that Mr Parker dipped *both* socks in the semolina.

'Ah,' he said as he pulled them on. 'That's much better.'

# My Best Fiend

## Sheila Lavelle

I was clearing out all the junk which had been shoved to the back of the art cupboard when I came across an old battered tin. I heaved it out and looked at the label and it said Cow Gum. I laughed and showed it to Angela.

'I wonder if that's for sticking cows,' I said. Then I started to put it away again on one of the shelves but Angela leaned over and took it out of my hands. Her face had sort of lighted up and I could see that she'd had one of her wicked ideas.

'What are you doing?' I asked anxiously. Angela found a stick and prised off the lid of the tin and we both looked inside. A thick layer of glue lay at the bottom, all sticky and shiny like varnish. Angela gazed at it for a minute, then she skipped away across the room with the tin in her hands. She stopped beside Miss Bennett's chair and started to dip the stick in the glue. I gave a shriek of horror.

'Angela! Don't!' I pleaded. 'Not Miss Bennett's chair!'

Angela turned and waved the stick at me. 'You're right,' she whispered hoarsely. 'I think I'll use it on a pig instead.' She crossed the room quickly, and before I could even try to stop her she had scraped out a big dollop of glue and spread it all over the seat of Laurence Parker's chair.

She pushed the tin of glue back in the cupboard just in time because at that moment the bell rang for the end of break and the other children started to come back into the classroom. That nosy Delilah Jones began to wrinkle her face and sniff as soon as she came into the room.

'What's that funny smell?' she asked. But Angela only shrugged her shoulders and looked blank, and I turned my back and went on putting all the stuff back in the cupboard. I didn't know what else to do.

When I had finished I went back to my place and sat down. I had a quick peep at Laurence Parker's chair and you couldn't tell there was glue on it at all. It only looked a bit more shiny than usual. Then I saw Laurence Parker come into the room so I put my head inside my desk because I just couldn't bear to watch him sit down.

I knew Miss Bennett had come in because all the chattering suddenly stopped and I heard everybody scuttling to their places.

'We're going to do some spelling now,' came Miss Bennett's voice. 'Take out your green spelling books, please, everybody. You may have five minutes to revise the twenty words we did last week, and then I'll test you on them.'

I grabbed my spelling book and when I put down my desk lid I saw that Laurence Parker was sitting in his place next to me and he hadn't noticed a thing. I looked over my shoulder, but Angela had her head down over her book and didn't look up.

It was all quiet for a few minutes while everybody except me practised their words and then Miss Bennett stood up.

'We'll start with the front row,' she said. 'I'll ask each of you to spell one word for me. Now, Delilah. You're first. Your word is, enough.'

And that awful Delilah Jones leaped up, looking all smug and pleased with herself. 'E-N-O-U-G-H,' she said, and Miss Bennett smiled at her and said, 'Well done,' and you should have seen Delilah Jones smirking all over her silly face.

Well, it went all the way along the front row and then all the way along the next row and then it was our row and I started to get that horrible feeling in my stomach that's called butterflies and I don't know why it's called getting butterflies because I think it feels more like great big creepy crawly caterpillars. And it was my turn at last and Miss Bennett said, 'Pneumonia, Charlotte,' and it was the hardest word on the list and I should have known Miss Bennett would save that one for me. Of course I knew how to spell it. But how could I think straight? How could anybody think straight if they knew that it was Laurence Parker's turn next and he was sitting there glued to his seat?

I stood up quickly. 'New what?' I said stupidly, and Miss Bennett's mouth went all squeezed up at the corners as if she was sucking a lemon.

'Pneumonia,' she said again.

'Um, er, N-E-W . . .' I began and Laurence Parker gave a snigger.

'Sit down, Charlotte,' said Miss Bennett crossly. 'It's obvious you don't know it. You must write it out three times in your book and learn it for next week. Perhaps Laurence Parker can do better. Laurence? Pneumonia, please.'

There was a sort of horrible clatter as Laurence Parker got to his feet and I didn't know where to look because of course his chair was stuck firmly to the seat of his trousers and had got up with him. His face went all red and he swung around to try to see what was the matter, but that only made things worse because the legs of the chair crashed into the desk behind. Miss Bennett's face went as black as thunder and everybody stared like anything and there were a few smothered giggles but nobody dared laugh out loud.

'What on earth are you doing, boy?' snapped Miss Bennett and Laurence Parker started twisting about and trying to pull himself free but the chair was well and truly stuck.

'Laurence Parker! Come here AT ONCE!' shouted Miss Bennett. 'I will not tolerate this sort of clowning

during my lessons!'

Laurence Parker hunched his shoulders and shuffled forward to the front of the class, clutching the chair to his bottom with his hands. He looked a bit like a fat old tortoise with its house on its back.

'I . . . I seem to have got stuck,' he stammered miserably, and Miss Bennett clucked and tutted and fussed. Then she put one hand on his shoulder and the other on the back of the chair and pulled.

There was a dreadful ripping noise and there stood Miss Bennett looking a bit surprised with the chair in her hand and hanging from the chair was a big piece of grey material. And there stood Laurence Parker looking even more surprised with a great big ragged hole in the seat of his trousers and you could see his blue and red striped Marks and Spencers underwear. Everybody stared in horror and the whole room went dead quiet and all you could hear was people breathing and that was when I started to laugh.

It wouldn't have been so bad if it had been a quiet little giggle, or a subdued sort of chuckle, but it wasn't. It was a horrible loud cackle. My dad says that when I laugh I sound like an old hen laying an egg. And I always seem to laugh at the wrong time and in the wrong place and sometimes it gets me into terrible trouble but I can't help it. Like the time at the vicar's garden party when Miss Menzies sneezed and her false teeth flew out and landed in the bowl of fruit punch. And that other time when we went to my Auntie Fiona's wedding up in Gateshead and my grandad trod on the end of the bride's long white veil as she was walking down the aisle and yanked it clean off her head and I laughed so much that I was sent out of the church and had to wait outside in the car so I missed the whole thing.

Anyway, Laurence Parker looked so funny standing there with that great hole in his trousers that if I hadn't laughed I'd have burst. My eyes streamed with tears and this time it was no use stuffing my hanky in my mouth because it only made me choke and laugh even more. And then of course when I started laughing like that it set everybody else off as well and soon the whole class was laughing like anything and you should have heard the din.

Miss Bennett started to thump on her desk with her fist and I knew I was in bad trouble because she only does that when she's really mad. And when I saw the way she was glaring at me I wished I hadn't laughed so much because of course that was what made her think it was me who had been messing about with the rotten old glue.

'There is glue on this chair,' said Miss Bennett, sort of quietly and ominously. 'And I don't have to ask who is responsible for this outrage.' Her eyes bored into me and I felt my face go scarlet. 'There were only two people left in this room at break time, and one of them has guilt written all over her face.' Miss Bennett turned to Laurence Parker, who had backed up against the wall to hide his underwear and was standing there looking daggers at me.

'Laurence,' she said, quite gently. 'You had better go and wait in the boys' changing room. I'm going to phone your mother and ask her to bring you a spare pair of trousers.' Then she turned back to me and her voice would have frozen the Sahara Desert. 'Charlotte Ellis, you will stay behind after school this afternoon. You and I must have a very serious talk.'

Well, of course I sort of hoped that Angela would stand up and confess, but I must admit I wasn't all that surprised when she didn't because I know what she's like. And I didn't get a single chance to speak to her on her own for the rest of that day, as she had to stay indoors again at lunch time because of her sore throat. So when four o'clock came everybody went home and I had to stay behind and get told off, and it was awful because Miss Bennett went on and on at me until I thought she'd never stop and all I could do was stand there and say nothing because of course she knew that it could only have been me or Angela and I couldn't tell on my friend, could I? Even if she did deserve it.

# Hop o' my Thumb

### René Goscinny

Our teacher told us that the Head was leaving, he was going to retire. We've been getting some fantastic celebrations ready at school, it's going to be like Prizegiving Day and all the mothers and fathers will come, and there'll be chairs in the Hall, and armchairs for the Head and the teachers, and decorations and a platform for the entertainment, which will be given by us boys.

Each class is doing something. The big ones are going to do gymnastics: they all climb on top of each other and the one on top waves a little flag and the audience clap. They did that last year on Prizegiving Day and it was absolutely great, though right at the end the flag bit didn't quite come off because they fell down before they could wave it. The class next above us is going to do folk-dancing, all dressed up in peasant costumes with clogs, and they stand in a circle and stamp about the platform in their clogs, only instead of waving a flag they wave hankies and shout 'Yoohoo!' They did that last year too; it wasn't as good as the

gymnastics display but they didn't fall down. Another class is singing *Nymphs and Shepherds* and an old boy of the school is going to make a speech of congratulations and tell us it was all because of the Head's good advice he grew to manhood and got to be Town Clerk.

Our part of the entertainment was going to be great. Our teacher told us we were going to act a play – a real play like in the theatre and on the television.

The play is called *Hop o' my Thumb and Puss in Boots*, and we had our first rehearsal at school today. Our teacher was giving out the parts. Geoffrey came dressed up as a cowboy just in case, his Dad is very rich and gives him lots of things, but our teacher wasn't all that keen on Geoffrey's get-up.

'Geoffrey, I've already told you I don't like you coming to school in fancy dress,' she said. 'Anyway, there aren't any cowboys in this play.'

'No cowboys?' said Geoffrey. 'What a lousy play!' and

our teacher made him stand in the corner.

The play has a very complicated story and I didn't understand it too well when our teacher explained it. I know there's Hop o' my Thumb looking for his brothers and he meets Puss in Boots and there's the Marquis of Carabas and an ogre who wants to eat Hop o' my Thumb's brothers and Puss in Boots helps Hop o' my Thumb and the ogre gets beaten and he turns nice and I think at the end he doesn't eat Hop o' my Thumb's brothers after all and everyone is happy and they have something else to eat instead.

'Now then,' said our teacher, 'who will be Hop o' my Thumb?'

'Me, miss,' said Cuthbert. 'It's the main part and I'm top of the class.' Which was true. Cuthbert really is top of the class and teacher's pet and a rotten sport who's always crying and he wears glasses and you can't thump him because of the glasses.

'You've got a nerve!' said Eddie. 'Watching you act Hop o' my Thumb will be like watching me do embroidery.' And Cuthbert started to cry and our teacher sent Eddie to stand in the corner along with Geoffrey.

'Now I want an ogre,' said our teacher. 'The Ogre who wants to eat Hop o' my Thumb.' I suggested Alec for the ogre, because he's so fat and he eats all the time. But Alec didn't fancy the idea, he looked at Cuthbert and he said, 'I'm not eating him!' It's the first time I ever knew Alec not want to eat something, but I suppose the idea of eating Cuthbert isn't exactly appetising. Cuthbert was upset because Alec didn't want to eat him. 'Take that back or I shall tell my parents and get you expelled!' Cuthbert shouted.

'Silence!' shouted our teacher. 'Alec, you can be the crowd of villagers, and you can be prompter too and whisper the words to your friends during the performance.' Alec liked the idea of prompting us, like when we're called up to the blackboard to answer questions. He took a biscuit out of his pocket and put it in his mouth and said, 'Sure thing!'

'What an expression!' said our teacher. 'Please speak correctly!'

'Sure thing, miss,' said Alec, and our teacher sighed, deeply. She does look awfully tired these days.

First choice for Puss in Boots was Max. Our teacher told him he'd have a lovely costume, with a sword and whiskers and a tail: Max liked the idea of the lovely costume and the whiskers and specially the sword, but he was dead against having any tail. 'I'd look like a monkey!' he said.

'Well, that won't be anything new,' said Jeremy, and Max kicked Jeremy, and Jeremy thumped Max, and the teacher put them both in the corner and told me I would be Puss in Boots and if I didn't like it that was just too bad, because she was getting fed up with the lot of us and she felt really sorry for our parents who had the job of bringing us up and if we carried on like this we should finish up in jail and she was sorry for the warders too.

After Rufus had been cast as the ogre and Matthew as the Marquis of Carabas, our teacher gave us some typewritten sheets of paper with the words we had to say. She realised there were lots of people standing in the corner by now, so she told them to come back and help Alec be the crowd of villagers. Alec wasn't too pleased, he wanted to be the crowd all on his own, but our teacher told him to be quiet. 'Right, let's start,' said our teacher. 'Read your parts carefully. Cuthbert, this is what you do: you come on stage, you're in despair, it's the middle of the forest and you're looking for your brothers. Then you meet Nicholas, who is Puss in Boots. Then the rest of you in the crowd all say together, "Why, that's Hop o' my Thumb and Puss in Boots!" Off you go!'

We went and stood in front of the blackboard. I'd stuck a ruler in my belt to pretend it was the sword and Cuthbert began to read his part. 'My brothers,' he said, 'oh, where are my poor brothers?' 'My brothers,' shouted Alec, 'oh, where are my poor brothers?'

'Whatever do you think you're doing, Alec?' asked our teacher.

'I'm the prompter so I'm prompting, that's all,' said Alec.

'Please, miss,' said Cuthbert, 'when Alec prompts he blows biscuit crumbs all over my glasses so I can't see and I'm going to tell my parents!' And Cuthbert took off his glasses to wipe them, so Alec seized the oppor-

59

tunity and thumped him.

'Go on, punch his nose!' shouted Eddie. Cuthbert started howling and crying. He said he was dreadfully unhappy and we wanted to kill him, and he rolled about the floor. Max, Jeremy and Geoffrey started being the crowd and shouting, 'Why, it's Hop o' my Thumb and Puss in Boots!' I was fighting Rufus; I had my ruler and he had a penholder, and the rehearsal was going brilliantly when all of a sudden our teacher shouted, 'That will do! Go back to your places! We shall not be acting this play at the celebrations after all. I'm not letting the Head see a performance like this!'

We all stood there with our jaws dropping.

It's the first time we ever heard our teacher say she was going to give the Head a punishment.

# The Name is Billy Molloy

### Kathryn Cave

The name is Billy Molloy.

On the day the story begins, a nine-year-old boy called Donald was sitting in a classroom. Not alone, naturally. There were thirty-three other people in the room with him. Thirty-two of these were fellow members of Class Three, among them Donald's friends Mark and Jamie. The thirty-third was their teacher, Mrs Augusta Bannerman. She was not doing anything extraordinary, just glaring in her usual fashion at each and every member of the class simultaneously. She was the only teacher in the school who could do this. She had a wide-angled glare – something, Donald suspected, to do with the upswept glasses that covered her small fierce eyes.

Donald had nothing to feel guilty about – he had only been sitting in the classroom for five minutes, which wasn't long enough to do anything worth feeling guilty for – but he had the desperate feeling that if the bell didn't ring soon to call them to assembly, he was going to confess everything from having torn a page out of his English notebook three weeks earlier to make a paper aeroplane, right through to not having cleaned his teeth before school. Fortunately the bell rang.

It was Wednesday – Wednesday the eighth of May – so the whole school had assembly together. When Donald thought back about this later, as he often did, he could not remember a single respect in which the assembly was anything other than entirely ordinary. On that particular Wednesday the same sorts of things happened at assembly: announcements by Miss Andrews, the headmistress; a hymn, during which several of the infants generally burst into tears; a prayer, in the course of which one particular boy always said in a husky voice, 'I feel sick, Miss' and had to be led out. These were parts of the school's regular routine and when they happened Donald would look across at Jamie (they hadn't been allowed to sit next to one another since Mrs Bannerman took over Class Three at Christmas) and grin, provided Mrs Bannerman was not watching. Mrs Bannerman did not like boys grinning at each other, and Donald did his best to avoid giving offence.

After assembly, other ordinary things must have happened. There must have been Maths before playtime, and Mrs Bannerman's daily test of mental arithmetic at which it was impossible to do well. If you worked slowly and neatly, you couldn't finish. If you got everything finished and everything right, the only comment, written in ink the colour of dried blood, would be: 'I will not tolerate untidy work.' Mrs Bannerman did not believe in making things easy.

The point at which that particular Wednesday started being different from any other day did not come until 1.45 p.m. Even as late as 1.44, life for Donald still pursued its normal course.

What he was doing at that particular moment in history was inking in a skull and crossbones on his left wrist (this was the badge of the secret society he, Jamie and Mark had decided to form). Had he looked up (which he didn't, being far too busy) he would have seen a number of other unremarkable sights: Jamie, two tables away, scratching his head with the tip of his favourite pencil, something he often did when bored or sleepy; Clare biting off split ends; Mark trying to write his own name upside-down left-handed with his eyes closed (an accomplishment he believed would take him straight to the top of MI5 when he finally got it right); Mary, Mrs Bannerman's special pet, hunting up the sleeve of her cardigan for a lost handkerchief; Mrs Bannerman herself, short and fierce as an elderly dragon, turning her back on the class in order to roll down the blackboard to reveal the subject of this week's Special Project.

Donald saw none of this, however. One of the crossbones had started to turn into a tennis racquet. Donald continued to give it all his attention even when the swish of the board signalled that Special Project time was under way. But then Clare's elbow caught Donald sharply in the ribs, he lifted his head, and Wednesday split in two.

There, right across Mrs Bannerman's diagram of the solar system in big red letters all the way from Mars to Venus, somebody had written:

DOWN WITH TYRANTS
BILLY MOLLOY

The fuss that followed was something quite tremendous. There had been messages of one sort or another written on the board before:

CLARE 4 ROBBERT
JOHN LOVS MARY

Simple statements like this had appeared from time to time, to be punished by Mrs Bannerman with terrible ferocity. But there had never been a message like that. The spelling, the punctuation, the mysterious name at the end (there was no Billy Molloy in Class Three or in the whole school, so far as Donald was aware) put it in a class of its own.

Mrs Bannerman was in a state of shock. When she came round she conducted the inevitable investigation, dark eyes snapping: 'Stand up the person who is responsible for this outrage.'

No one stood up. The only person who showed any sign of life was Clare, who chose that moment to demonstrate her indifference to danger by asking what

'tyrants' meant.

Mary's guess ('It means teacher, doesn't it, Miss?') scarcely improved the situation. From that moment on she would never again be Mrs Bannerman's pet, however many times she might offer to carry out bags of fossils and rock samples to the staff car park in the evening. It was the end of an era.

Meanwhile the investigation continued. No one in Class Three admitted writing the message or knowing anyone called Billy Molloy. No one but Mary and Jamie put forward any theory about what 'tyrants' meant. (Jamie said he thought it might be a kind of fish).

From Mrs Bannerman's point of view it was extremely frustrating. The last thing she would have expected to find in Class Three was someone with the cunning and determination (not to mention the grasp of spelling and punctuation) to produce that elegant and economical slogan. DOWN WITH TEACHERS, now – that had come her way before, and DWON WITH TEECHER'S, too. But DOWN WITH TYRANTS! – Mrs Bannerman was baffled. Behind which of the ordinarily stupid faces in Class Three did the writer of that message lie concealed? She could not begin to imagine.

'What are tyrants, then,' asked Jamie on his way home, 'if they aren't fish after all?'

Donald gave the answer after a brief pause for thought. 'People who boss other people about and make them do things they don't want to. Like Hitler and Genghis Khan and people like that.' He didn't have to say, 'Like Mrs Bannerman.' For Class Three that went without saying.

Someone, however, took a different view.

The very day after he had first made his presence known, Billy Molloy struck again. This time no special skills were required to understand the message.

BANNERMAN MUST GO
REMEMBER BILLY MOLLOY

said the blackboard.

Mrs Bannerman looked from the board to the children, thin-lipped. Then she went to fetch Miss Andrews.

Miss Andrews – tall and vague and thin, serving out her last term before taking early retirement – looked at the message and then at Class Three. 'I hope none of you would write anything so unkind,' she said in her mild, serious voice.

'Oh no, Miss Andrews,' thirty-three voices replied in unison.

'Go on with your work, then, children.'

'Someone wrote it,' Mrs Bannerman pointed out. 'And I intend to find out who it was.'

Outside the classroom (Donald could hear through the half-open door) Miss Andrews suggested that the incident was best treated as a bad joke. If Mrs Bannerman felt unable to ignore it (Mrs Bannerman made it clear she could not), then perhaps she could take the wind out of the slogan-writer's sails by – well, perhaps by being a little more ready to make concessions to the children. They were only nine years old, after all. Miss Andrews was sure Mrs Bannerman would agree that allowances should be made.

Mrs Bannerman did not agree. On the contrary, she declared war outright on Billy Molloy. It was a war all the more bitter because it was waged against an invisible enemy. Because Mrs Bannerman had no means of identifying the culprit she proceeded as if each and every member of Class Three was guilty at the very least

68

of aiding and abetting Billy Molloy in his crimes. She prowled, she swooped, she pounced.

Before that first day was out, Mrs Bannerman had confiscated a lurex hair ribbon and a bottle of gold nail varnish from Clare and a bag of marshmallows from Mary (poor Mary, slow to realise that she was no longer a pet, had begun to eat them openly as usual during Bible Study). These forbidden objects were soon joined in Mrs Bannerman's bottom drawer by Mark's manual of secret codes, a broken water pistol that Jamie had been hoping to repair in a peaceful moment during 'Life in Ancient Rome', and a large rubber band with which Donald had certainly not been going to flick paper pellets at Jamie during silent reading.

In between confiscating everything she could lay her hands on, Mrs Bannerman spent a lot of time and effort sneaking back into the classroom during play-time. Donald and Jamie once came across her in the cloakroom on all fours, craning her neck round a coat rack to peer in through the classroom door. They crept away before she could see them, but they knew what she was up to. She was trying to catch Billy Molloy red-handed. She never did.

Donald's admiration for their unknown champion grew daily.

BANNERMAN OUT! OUT! OUT!

was the clarion call that greeted them on Friday after

lunch followed by:

## Go HoME BANNERMAN

the following Wednesday morning. The next message
(Thursday, after games) was perhaps a little general:

## FREEDOM FoR ALL!

but on the whole Donald gave it his approval, while on
Monday the writer was right back on target:

## BANNERMAN IS NO GOOD

The signature at the end of each message never varied:
it was always Billy Molloy.

It got even Mrs Bannerman down in the end. She
withdrew her application for Miss Andrews' post as
head teacher at St Matthew's. She applied for jobs at

other schools in the county, but without success. Perhaps word had got round and governing bodies were wary of taking on someone who was haunted by a private ghost.

The mental arithmetic tests got harder and harder, the messages in dried blood became more and more savage. Donald drew up a chart counting the number of days until the end of the summer term would set him free of Mrs Bannerman for ever.

In early July (still twelve days to go) Donald was waiting outside Miss Andrews' study with the register for Class Three. Someone was in the study talking to her, and he was too shy to knock. The door opened, and Miss Andrews came out, smiling her kind, serious smile. With her was a small man in a black suit.

'I will leave Donald to look after you, Michael,' she said. 'I will not be long. Donald, this is my brother, Father Andrews. I would like you to show him our roses, while I have a quick talk with the infants. I will let Mrs Bannerman know where you are.'

Donald and Father Andrews looked at the roses, which didn't take long, and then at each other.

Father Andrews had a round, mild face and gold-rimmed glasses. He didn't look in the least like Miss Andrews, but he talked to Donald in her voice. Once he got going, the words flowed in a soft Irish stream that left Donald very little to do but smile and give the occasional nod.

'My sister is being a long time,' said Father Andrews, flagging at last. 'She's always been the chatterbox of us two. You don't believe me, do you? I promise you, when she was your age, she was always in trouble for talking in class. And for other things too. The tricks she got up to, you wouldn't believe them. Not cruel, mind you. She always had the same kind heart, even then. I remember there was this child in her class, couldn't get anything right, fell over his feet, spelled his name backwards, daydreaming all the time, always in hot water one way or another, drove some of the teachers mad. He moved away or something in the end, I forget what, but Kathleen (that's my sister), she was always on his side, and after Billy left' – Donald froze as Father Andrews chuckled gently – 'these messages started appearing on the blackboards. All sorts of things they said. I won't go into it, but they got the teachers in a rage because they were all signed with that boy's name, and him long gone, and no way they could blame him for them.'

'What did you say his name . . .?' Donald didn't finish the question, but he had no need to. Father Andrews patted him gleefully on the shoulder and bent close to whisper:

'To this very day, I doubt if there's anyone but me and you, Donald, who knows that Kathleen Andrews was really Billy Molloy.'

It was a moment Donald was to remember for thirty years – maybe for sixty. Before he had to find something to say, Miss Andrews was back again. Father Andrews beamed at them both.

'Ah, Kathleen, Donald here has been entertaining me in fine style, and I'm sorry to have to part from him to take you out to lunch, but we shall have to look sharp or I'll miss my train back to London and then I'll miss my boat, and then where will I be? Goodbye, Donald, and thank you for looking after me so well.'

Twelve days later the term ended. Donald gave a shilling towards Miss Andrews' retirement present and he wished he could have given more. A lot of children and parents must have given money too, because on the last day of term Miss Andrews was presented with a gold clock in a glass case. She looked as vague as ever as she said goodbye to the school. There was no trace of Billy Molloy to be seen in her anywhere – no trace at all. She smiled her remote smile, picked up the gold clock in her arms, and walked out of Donald's life for ever.

# What's for Dinner?

### Robert Swindells

'It's Friday,' Sammy Troy complained. 'Fish and chip day. Why are we having shepherd's pie?'

'I don't know, do I?' said Jane. They were twins but Sammy was ten minutes younger and ten years dafter. Jane spent half her time at school keeping him out of trouble. She swallowed a forkful of the pie. 'It's very tasty anyway. Try it.'

Sammy tried it. It was good, but he wasn't going to admit it. He'd been looking forward to fish and chips and shepherd's pie just wasn't the same. He pulled a face.

'Pigfood.'

'Don't be silly,' said Jane, but she knew he would be. He usually was.

Sammy left most of his dinner, and in the playground afterwards he made up a rap. It was about the school cook, and it went like this:

'Elsie Brook is a useless cook
If you eat school dinners it's your hard luck

They either kill or make you ill
If the meat don't do it then the custard will.'

It wasn't true. Mrs Brook did good dinners, but the rap caught on and a long snake of chanting children wound its way about the playground with Sammy at its head. Jane didn't join in. She thought it was stupid and hoped Mrs Brook wouldn't hear it.

On Saturday, Sammy practised the rap with some of his friends. They meant to get it going again at break on Monday, but at the end of the morning assembly the Head said, 'I'm sorry to have to tell you all that our Mrs Brook was taken ill over the weekend and will not be here to cook for us this week.'

Some of the boys grinned and nudged one another. Sammy whispered in Jane's ear, 'She must've eaten some of that shepherd's pie.' Jane jabbed him with her elbow.

'However,' continued the Head, 'we are very lucky to have with us Mr Hannay, who will see to our meals till Mrs Brook returns. Mr Hannay is not only a first-class chef but an explorer as well. He has travelled as cook on a number of expeditions to remote regions, and is famous for his ability to produce appetising meals from the most unpromising ingredients.'

'He'll feel at home here, then,' muttered Sammy. 'We have the most unpromising ingredients in Europe.'

A chef, though! A first-class chef. Morning lessons seemed to drag forever. It felt like three o'clock when the buzzer went, though it was five to twelve as always. Hands were washed in two seconds flat, and everybody hurried along to the dining area which was filled with a delicious mouth-watering aroma. Snowy cloths covered all the tables, and on each table stood a little pot of flowers. 'Wow!' breathed Jeanette Frazer. 'It's like a posh restaurant.'

And the food. Oh, the food. First came a thick, fragrant soup which was green but tasted absolutely fantastic. To follow the soup there was a beautiful main course – succulent nuggets of tender white meat in a golden, spicy sauce with baby peas and crispy roast potatoes. And for pudding there were giant helpings of chocolate ice cream with crunchy bits in it.

Sammy licked the last smear of ice cream from his spoon, dropped the spoon in his dish, pushed the dish away and belched. Some of the boys giggled, but his sister glared at him across the table. Sammy smiled. 'Sorry, but what a meal, eh? What a stupendous pig-out. I'll probably nod off in biology this aft.'

He didn't though. Miss Corbishley didn't give him the chance. The class was doing pond life, and when they walked in the room the teacher said, 'Jane and Sammy Tory, take the net and specimen jar, go down to the pond and bring back some pond beetles and a waterboatman or two. Quickly now.'

The school pond lay in a hollow beyond the playing field. Rushes grew thickly round its marshy rim and there were tadpoles, newts and dragonflies as well as sticklebacks and the beetles they'd studied today. It was Sammy's favourite spot, but today all the creatures seemed to be in hiding. No dragonflies darted away as the twins waded through the reeds. No sticklebacks scattered like silver pins when Jane trawled the net through the pondweed, and when she lifted it out it was empty.

'Try again,' said Sammy. 'Faster.'

Jane sent the net swooping through the underwater forest, but all she got was a plume of weed.

'Everything seems to have gone,' she said. 'And Miss is waiting.'

'I know,' said Sammy. 'She'll think we've wagged off school.'

'Don't be ridiculous,' cried Miss Corbishley, when

Jane told her there was nothing in the pond. 'Only this morning Mr Hannay was saying what a well-stocked pond we have at Milton Middle.' The twins were sent to their seats in disgrace, while Jeanette Frazer and Mary Bain went to try their luck. Miss Corbishley made a giant drawing of a water boatman on the board and the children began copying it into their books.

'Hey, Jane!' hissed Sammy. His sister looked at him. He had a funny look on his face. 'I've just had a thought.'

'Congratulations,' she whispered. 'I knew you would some day.'

'No, listen. You know what Miss said, about Mr Hannay?'

'What about it?'

'He said the pond was well stocked, right? And now it isn't. And we had that fantastic dinner, only we didn't really know what it was?'

'What's dinner got to do with . . .?' Jane broke off and gazed at her brother. She shook her head. 'No, Sammy. No. That's sick. It's impossible.'

'Is it?' Sammy jabbed a finger at her. 'What was that soup, then? Green soup. And the meat. And those crunchy bits in the ice cream – what were they?'

Before Jane could reply, Jeanette and Mary came back with long faces and an empty jar.

Walking home that afternoon Jane said, 'It's a coinci-dence, that's all. It can't be true what you're thinking,

Sammy.' She wasn't sure though, and Sammy certainly wasn't convinced. 'I wonder what we'll get tomorrow?' he said.

Tuesday's dinner turned out to be every bit as delicious as Monday's. The twins had kept their suspicions to themselves, so there were no spoilt appetites as the children settled down to eat. Even Jane and Sammy felt better. After all, even Mr Hannay couldn't conjure food from an empty pond.

The soup was orange and there were no lumps in it. It had plenty of flavour though, and everybody enjoyed it. The main course was Italian – mounds of steaming pasta and a rich, meaty tomato sauce. 'If this is how they eat in Italy,' said Sammy, 'I'm off to live there.' He seemed to have forgotten about yesterday. Jane hadn't, but she knew macaroni when she saw it, and this was definitely macaroni.

Tuesday afternoon was C.D.T. with Mr Parker. When the kids arrived he was kneeling in front of his big cupboard, surrounded by a mountain of dusty old drawings, and broken models made from balsa wood and cardboard boxes. 'Lost something, sir?' asked Sammy.

Mr Parker nodded. 'I'm afraid I have, lad. I could've sworn they were in here.'

'What, sir?'

'Some pictures I did with a first-year class three, maybe four years ago. Collage pictures.'

'What are they, sir?'

'Oh, you know – you stick things on a sheet of paper to make a picture. Seashells, lentils, bits of macaroni. Any old rubbish you can find, really.'

Sammy gulped. 'Bits of macaroni, sir?'

'That's right.'

'Four years ago, sir?'

'Yes. I'm sure I saw them at the back of the cupboard quite recently and made a mental note to clear them out before the mice got to them.'

'Are there mice in your cupboard, sir?' There was a greenish tint to Sammy's face.

'Oh yes, lad. Mice, moths, woodlice, cockroaches. The odd rat, probably. It's a miniature zoo, this cupboard.'

Sammy didn't enjoy C.D.T. that afternoon. He couldn't concentrate. He kept picturing old Hannay in his blue-and-white striped apron, rooting through Parker's cupboard. When he glanced across at Jane he thought she looked unwell. He wondered how Mrs Brook was getting along, and when the boys did the rap at break he didn't join in.

On Wednesday, Jane and Sammy decided they wouldn't eat school lunch unless they knew what it was. Sammy said, 'How do we find out what it is?'

'We ask,' Jane told him. At eleven o'clock she stuck her hand up and asked to go to the toilet but went to the kitchen instead. Mr Hannay wasn't there, but Mrs

Trafford was. 'Where's Mr Hannay?' asked Jane. She hoped he'd left, but Mrs Trafford said, 'He's just slipped along to the gym, dear. Why – who wants him?'

'Oh, nobody,' said Jane. 'I was wondering what's for dinner, that's all.'

'Opek,' said Mrs Trafford.

'Pardon?' said Jane.

'Opek. It's a very old oriental dish, Mr Hannay says. Very nice.'

Opek turned out to be a grey, porridge mush. It didn't look all that promising, but it was probably what ancient grub was supposed to look like and it tasted fine. Everybody was enjoying it till Gaz Walker fished a small flat rectangular object from his plate and held it up.

'Here,' he complained. 'Why is there a Size 4 tag in my dinner?'

'Let's have a look.' Jane took the tag and examined it. It looked like the sort of tag you'd find inside a shoe. 'Opek,' she murmured, wondering why Mr Hannay had been in the gym when he was supposed to be cooking. 'Opek.' An idea formed in her head and sank slowly into her stomach where it lay like a lead weight. She put the tag on the rim of her plate and sat back with her hands across her stomach. All round the table, kids stopped eating and watched her.

'What's up, Jane?' Sammy's voice was husky.

'Opek,' whispered Jane. 'I think I know what it

means.'

'What does it mean?' asked Jeanette, who had almost cleared her plate.

'I think it's initials,' said Jane. 'Standing for Old P.E. Kit.'

The peace of the dining area was shattered by cries of revulsion and the scrape and clatter of chairs as everybody on Jane's table stampeded for the door. The kids at the other tables watched till they'd gone, then lowered their heads and went on eating opek.

Sometimes two people can keep a secret, but never ten. There were ten kids at Jane and Sammy's table, and so the secret came out. Nobody went in to dinner on Thursday. Nobody. At twelve o'clock Mr Hannay raised the hatch and found himself gazing at twelve empty tables. He frowned at his watch. Shook it. Raised it to his ear. At five-past twelve he took off his apron and went to see the Head. They stood at the Head's window, looking towards the playing field. All the children were there, and some seemed to be eating the grass. 'Good lord,' sighed the Head. 'What did you cook, Hannay?'

'Epsatsc,' said the chef.

'Never heard of it,' said the head. 'What is it?'

'Traditional Greek dish,' said Hannay smoothly, easily fooling the Head. Jane, who'd got the word from Mrs Trafford, wasn't fooled. 'Epsatsc,' she said, grimly, leaning on a goalpost. 'Erasers, pencil shavings and the school cat.'

On Friday everybody brought sandwiches but they needn't have, because Hannay had gone and Mrs Brook was back. When they spotted her crossing the play-ground at five-to-nine the kids cheered. Mrs Brook, who was the sentimental type, had to wipe her eyes before she could see to hang up her coat. The kids chucked their butties in the bin and Sammy's rap was dead.

Dinner wasn't fish and chips, but there were no complaints. Everybody tucked in with gusto – even Sammy. The snowy cloths had gone and there were no flowers, but there was something else instead. Contentment. You could feel it all around.

And so the school week drew to a close. Everybody relaxed. The work was done. The weekend, bright with promise, lay ahead. At half-past three the kids spilled whooping into the yard and away down the drive. Jane and Sammy, in no rush, strolled behind. At the top of the drive stood the gardener, looking lost. Sammy grinned. 'What's up, Mr Tench?' The gardener lifted his cap and scratched his head. 'Nay,' he growled. 'There were a pile of nice, fresh horse manure here this morning and it's gone.'

The twins exchanged glances. Mrs Brook was coming down the drive. They ran to her. 'Mrs Brook!' cried Sammy. 'That Mr Hannay – he has left, hasn't he?'

The cook nodded. 'Yes, dear, I'm afraid he has but don't worry – he left me his recipe book, and you know it's just amazing the meals you can get out of stuff you find lying around.'

# The Hidden Horse

## Martin Waddell

'I've got it!' said Harriet.

'Got what?' said Anthea.

'Your horse,' said Harriet. 'It's a very nice one. You're going to like it.'

'Where is it?' said Anthea.

'Hidden!' said Harriet, blowing an extra big bubble.

'Hidden *where?*' asked Anthea, as they turned in through the gates of Slow Street Primary.

'Here,' said Harriet. 'I hid it here last night.'

'In school?' said Anthea.

'That's right,' said Harriet. 'Hidden where no one will find it.'

'But . . .' said Anthea.

'Good morning, Anthea. Good morning, Harriet,' said Miss Granston, with a sinking heart. Her heart always sank when she saw Harriet. This time it sank even further.

Harriet was carrying a small sack.

Miss Granston knew better than to ask what was in the sack. Instead she headed for her office, and the

Tonic Wine, which she kept on the premises for medicinal purposes.

'Hidden where?' asked Anthea, as they turned in through the door of P7.

'I'll show you at break!' said Harriet.

'Morning, everyone!' said Mr Tiger and Mr Cousins, breezing into the staff room.

Nobody said good morning back.

Mr Tiger knew the signs. He turned round to go out again, quickly, but Mr Cousins was too quick for him.

'What's up?' Mr Cousins asked.

'Tennis balls in my tuba!' said Miss Tremloe dramatically. 'That's what's up!'

'Football jerseys in the kitchen dishwasher!' said Miss Barton.

'There's a trampoline in the toilet!' said Mrs Whitten, who had bounced on it when she least expected to, and hadn't quite recovered.

Miss Ash didn't say anything, because she didn't know how to put it politely, but she had stepped in something in the Assembly Hall – something which shouldn't have been there.

'Ah-ha!' said Mr Tiger, who felt he ought to say something, but was far too wise to commit himself.

'Something's afoot!' said Mr Cousins, getting interested.

'Something's very smelly!' said Miss Barton.

Miss Ash moved away from her.

'A smelly foot, perhaps?' said Mr Tiger, trying to cheer everybody up, but nobody smiled.

Miss Ash blushed crimson to the roots of her hair and went off to the toilet where she tripped on the trampoline and spilled her eau-de-cologne.

'What can be at the bottom of it all?' cried Miss Wilson, nervously.

'Harriet,' said Anthea. 'Harriet? Can I see it now, before the bell, please, Harriet?'

'See what?' said Charlie Green, pricking up his ears.

'*Nothing*,' said Harriet quickly.

'Oh yes there is!' said Charlie Green.

'Oh no there isn't!' said Harriet,

'Oh yes there is!' said Charlie.

'Oh no there isn't!' said Harriet.

'Oh yes . . . ARUUUGLUG!' said Charlie, as Harriet's sack went over his head. It had started off half full of oats, and now the other half was full of Charlie.

'Anybody else want to argue?' asked Harriet, looking round at Marky and Fat Olga and Sylvester Wise and the rest of P7, who had retreated to the far end of the classroom.

'There's nothing to see,' said Harriet. 'And no one's going to see it. Agreed, Charlie?'

'ARGLUG!' said Charlie emerging from the sack.

'He agrees!' said Harriet, going to her desk. She removed the pin Fat Olga had left for her to sit on, and put it on Miss Wilson's chair instead.

Anthea sat down next to her friend.

'Harriet?' she said. 'Harriet, you know the *Nothing* I'm not going to see? When can I *not* see it?'

The Anti-Harriet League held an emergency meeting behind the tuck shop at break.

'There *is* something!' said Charlie Green. 'Harriet's hidden something, and we ought to know what it is.'

'Before she gets us with it,' said Sylvester Wise.

'How do we know she's going to get us?' asked Marky.

'Because she always does,' said Sylvester.

'What about the Clue?' asked Charlie.

'What Clue?' asked Fat Olga.

'Oats,' said Charlie.

'Not much of a Clue, if you ask me,' said Marky, but he was wrong.

'There!' said Harriet.

'Where?' said Anthea. She could see where Harriet was pointing, but she couldn't see any horse.

'In there,' said Harriet, and she opened the cupboard door.

Lots of things usually lived in the cupboard. Sticks and staves and ropes and balls and bats and the trampoline and tennis racquets and whistles and the deckchair Mr Tiger used when refereeing matches from the centre spot. All these things should have been there, but they weren't. Instead there was a horse.

'OOOOOOH!' gasped Anthea.

The horse blinked sleepily. It was a dreamy horse, by nature, and the cupboard was next to the pipes, so it was hot. The horse was used to cold fields and commons. It hadn't been so comfortable for years, but it was still pleased to see its whistling friend. It nuzzled Harriet gently.

'There you are, horse,' said Harriet. 'Oats!' She hung the sack up on the inside of the door, where Mr Tiger's umpiring jacket should have been. It wasn't there now, because the horse was sitting on it.

The horse started to eat. It hadn't had a bite since last night's performance at the Circus, and it felt very peckish.

'Isn't it great?' said Harriet. 'The games cupboard is just right for keeping it in.'

'How did you get it in?' asked Anthea, looking nervously at the horse. It had big teeth.

'I had to shove it a bit,' said Harriet. 'Sort of sideways, and round a bit, and in.' She paused expectantly. She was waiting for Anthea to say what a nice horse it was and thank-you-very-much, but Anthea didn't.

'It's big,' Anthea said doubtfully.

'Not very,' said Harriet.

'I wanted a little one,' said Anthea.

'It was the smallest one I could find,' said Harriet, sounding hurt.

'It's not much use to me in a cupboard, is it?' said Anthea. 'I can't ride it in a cupboard.'

'You couldn't fall off it either,' said Harriet. 'There isn't room.'

The horse gave a gentle, contented whinny. Anthea, who had put out her hand to stroke it, stepped back hurriedly.

'You can sit on it in the cupboard,' said Harriet. 'You can practise sitting on it safely.'

'What about exercise, Harriet?' asked Anthea from a safe distance. 'Horses need exercise.'

Harriet thought about it.

'You want to *ride* it?' she said. 'Not just *sit* on it?'

'I want to ride it after I've sat on it,' said Anthea.

'Up and down, jumping over things?' said Harriet.

Anthea nodded.

'What are we going to do, Harriet?' she asked.

'Leave it to me!' said Harriet.

Night fell on Slow Street. The pale moon climbed high above the gasometer and stuck there, like a boiled egg in a cup, and the only sound was the creaking of a door marked:-

## MISS C. GRANSTON M.A.
## PRINCIPAL

as Ethel Bunch the Cleaning Lady crept through it, on her way to clean the Tonic Wine.

Ethel removed the Tonic Wine from the filing cabinet, where it was filed under 'T', and settled in Miss Granston's chair, easing off her cleaning slippers and dropping them into her bucket. She settled her mop against the radiator to dry, and put her feet up on Miss Granston's desk, beside the Class Registers.

The clock on the wall ticked softly behind her, and the level of the Tonic Wine fell as Ethel's spirits rose.

Ethel was dreaming of Robert, the Spanish Postman. He said he was Spanish, and Ethel believed him, because he had dark flashing eyes and carried garlic in his little red van. Robert had kissed her twice on Tuesday and was about to do it again in her dreams when . . .

*Clip-clop-clip-clop-clip-clop.*

Ethel opened one eye, and then the other.

*Clip-clop-clip-clop-clip-clop.*

Perhaps it was too much Tonic Wine, but she could have sworn she'd heard . . .

*Clip-clop-clip-clop-clip-clop.*

She *had* heard.

Ethel went rigid.

*Clip-clop-clip-clop-clip-clop.*

Hoofbeats ... hoofbeats drumming down the corridor.

Ethel knew what it was, of course.

She had been born and reared in Slow Street, and Ethel's old Dad had told her tales: Tales of the Slow Street Phantom.

*Clip-clop-clip-clop-clip-clop.*

Ethel shrank to the floor, as the sound of the ghostly hoofbeats echoed round her.

The Phantom ... the ghastly headless spectre which haunted Slow Street, hunting through the night for his lost love, who had died of a broken heart in the farmhouse ... the farmhouse that had once been on the site where now stood ...

*Slow Street Primary School.*

'Aaaaah!' screamed Ethel, curling up under the desk. She stuck Miss Granston's waste-paper basket over her head. It was full of old exam papers and orange pips, but Ethel didn't mind. Anything, anything to drown the dreaded:

*Clip-clop-clip-clop-clip-clop.*

The ghostly hoofbeats pounded past the door of the Principal's Office. Then they faded away down the corridor, towards the Gym, leaving Ethel pale and trembling inside the waste-paper basket, with pips up her nose.

Scooping up her mop and bucket, she ran barefoot from Slow Street School – into the arms of a passing policeman. It was a horrible experience for them both, because she still had her head in the waste-paper basket, and as a result she couldn't see whose arms she was in.

She thought it was the phantom.

Ethel hit him with her mop, banged him with her bucket, and got arrested for *Assaulting a Policeman in*

*the Course of His Duty.*

Within hours, the World knew Ethel's story . . . or if not the World, at least the Staff and Pupils of Slow Street Primary School, where the Phantom lurked.